First published 1991 by
Walker Books Ltd, 87 Vauxhall Walk
London SE11 5HJ

First printed 1991
Printed and bound in Hong Kong
by Dai Nippon Printing Co. (H.K.) Ltd.

British Library Cataloguing in Publication Data
The New Walker Bear Anthology vol. 2
Children's literature in English – Anthologies
I. Title
820.809282

ISBN 0-7445-2119-X

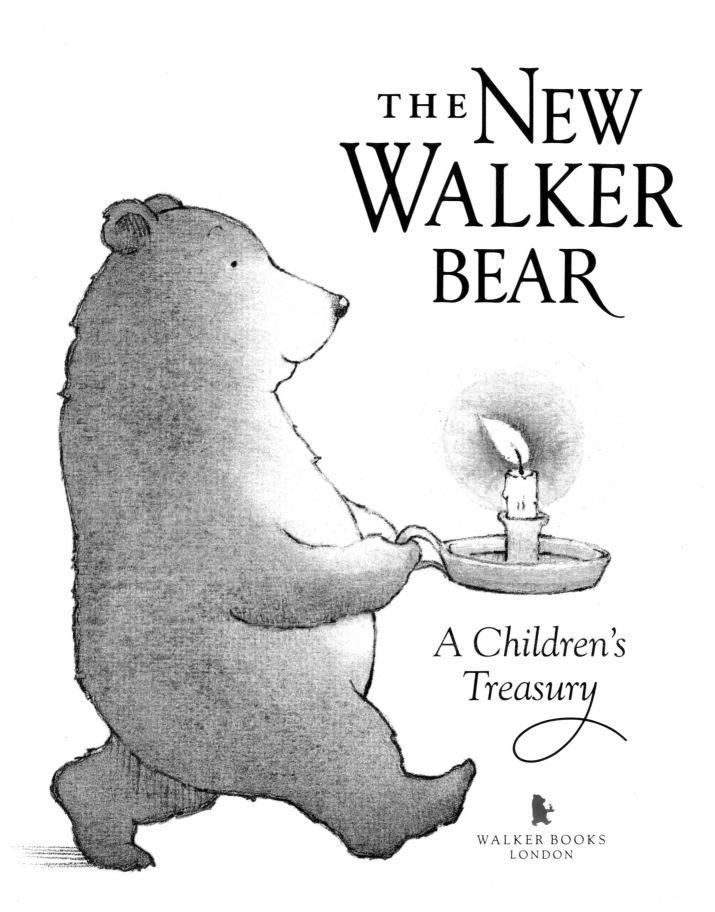

THE NEW WALKER BEAR

A Children's Treasury

WALKER BOOKS
LONDON

CONTENTS

This book is a second collection of the Walker Bear's favourite stories and pictures – thirty-five books or bits of books all wrapped up in one. It is a sampling of the work of some of the world's finest writers and illustrators for children, and as such truly deserves to be called a children's treasury. Each author and illustrator in the book speaks or sees in a purely individual way. Yet all together they create one image of the glittering joys of childhood, for the pleasure of children and hopefully the rest of the family as well.

The original books from which this anthology has been compiled can be bought in bookshops or borrowed from the library – all you need to know is the name of the book, and who wrote it and who drew the pictures. And of course there are many other books to look for and enjoy by the same authors and illustrators. This children's treasury can be the beginning of a greater treasure-hunt. The Walker Bear, who keeps saying you can't beat a good story, is never happier than when looking for another good book.

The Walker Bear welcomes you to this new collection and as always hopes you have a truly wonderful time.

Goodbye!

I LIKE BOOKS

by Anthony Browne

I like books.
Funny books
and scary books.
Fairy tales
and nursery
rhymes.
Comic books
and colouring books.
Fat books
and thin books.
Books about
dinosaurs,
and books about
monsters.
Counting books
and alphabet books.

Books about space,
and books
about pirates.

Song books
and strange books.

Yes,
I really
do like
books.

10

WHEN THE WALRUS COMES
by *Chris Riddell*

It's always fun when the walrus comes to visit. It's fun when we do things and fun when we don't. One day we packed our bags and set sail in the Phoebe McBean. We sailed up and down and round and round until we came to an island where monkeys live. The monkeys helped us unpack and they helped us eat our sandwiches. They showed us all the things which monkeys like to do, like climbing trees and swinging on vines and hanging upside down.

And we showed them what we like to do, like standing on our heads and doing cartwheels and pulling silly faces. Then the walrus played to us on the curly-wurly Eudophone, and we had fun being noisy. And we had fun being quiet when the moon and stars came out. That's how it is – it's always fun when the walrus comes to visit.

Rosie's Babies

by
Martin
Waddell

illustrated by
Penny
Dale

Mum was putting the baby to bed and Rosie said, "I've got two babies and you've only got one."
"Two, including you," said Mum.
"I'm not a baby, I'm four years old," said Rosie.
"Tell me about your babies," Mum said.

And Rosie said, "My babies live in a bird's nest and they are nearly as big as me. They go out in the garden all by themselves and sometimes they make me cross!"
"Do they?" said Mum.
"Yes. When they do silly things!" said Rosie.
"What silly things do they do?" asked Mum.

And Rosie said, "My babies climbed a big mountain. That was silly, because they couldn't get down. They jumped, and they bumped on their bottoms!"
"Silly babies," said Mum.
"Did they hurt themselves?"

And Rosie said,
"One of my babies
hurt her knee.
I bandaged it up and
she cried and I said
'Never mind'
because I am kind."
"I'm sure you are," said
Mum. "What else do
your babies do?"

And Rosie said,
"My babies drive cars
that are real ones
and lorries and
dumpers and boats.
My babies are very
good drivers."
"What do your babies
like doing best?"
asked Mum.

And Rosie said,
"My babies like swings
and rockers and
dinosaurs. They go
to the park when it's
dark and there are no
mums and dads who
can see, only me!"
"Gracious!" said Mum.
"Aren't they scared?"

And Rosie said,
"My babies are scared
of the big dogs,
but I'm not. I go
GRRRRRRRRRRRRR!
and frighten the big
dogs away."
"They are not
very scared then?"
said Mum.
"My babies know
I will look after
them," said Rosie.

"I'm their mum."
"How do you look
after them?"
Mum asked.

And Rosie said,
"I make their teas
and I tell them
stories and I take
them for walks and
I talk to them and
I tell them that I
love them."

"That's a good way
to look after
babies!" said Mum.
"Do you make
them nice things
to eat, like pies?"

And Rosie said,
"My babies make
their own pies, but
they never eat them."
"What do they eat?"
asked Mum.

And Rosie thought and thought and thought and then Rosie said, "My babies have gone to bed." "Just like this one," said Mum. "I don't want to talk about my babies any more because they are asleep," said Rosie.

And Rosie said, "My babies eat apples and apples and apples all the time. And grapes and pears but they don't like the pips." "Most babies don't," said Mum. "Are you going to tell me more about your babies?"

"I don't want them to wake up, or they'll cry." "We could talk very softly," said Mum. "Yes," said Rosie. "What will we talk about?" asked Mum.

And Rosie said,

"ME!"

THE WHISTLING PIGLET

by Dick King-Smith
illustrated by Norman Johnson

"Who's that whistling?" said Mumpig. "What an awful noise!"
"It's Henry," said nine of her ten spotty piglets.
Henry, the tenth piglet, didn't say anything because he was busy whistling. He pursed up his little mouth and whistled like a blackbird.

"And it's not an awful noise!" cried his brothers and sisters. "It's brill! It's catchy! It makes your feet itch!" and they all began to dance round Henry.
"How shameful!" grunted Mumpig. "To think that I am the mother of the world's first whistling piglet!"

And she was not the only mother on the farm who did not like what Henry was doing. "Who's that whistling?" mooed the cows. "What a fearful row!"
"Who's that whistling?" bleated the sheep. "What a dreadful din!"
"Who's that whistling?" cackled the hens. "What a frightful racket!"
But their young ones did not agree. "It's not a fearful row!" cried the calves and, "It's not a dreadful din!" cried the lambs and, "It's not a frightful racket!" cried the baby chicks. And they all of them said, "It's brill! It's catchy! It makes your feet itch!" and they all began to dance. As well as being brill and catchy and making their feet itch, there was one particular tune that Henry sometimes whistled that made all the young animals feel that they would run after him, wherever he went. It was the tune of the song whose words go like this:

Come follow, follow, follow,
Follow, follow, follow me.
Whither shall I follow,
follow, follow,
Whither shall I follow,
follow thee?
To the greenwood,
to the greenwood,
To the greenwood,
greenwood tree.

16

Every time Henry whistled that tune, the calves would break out of their pens; and the lambs would jump out of their fields; and the chicks would flutter out of their runs; and all would rush to follow Henry.

How angry the farmer was!

Almost every day he had to catch all the young animals and put them back in their proper places.

"And all because of that whistling piglet!" he said to his wife and his little daughter, "What a horrible hullabaloo!"

"It is!" said his wife.

"It's not!" said his little daughter. "It's brill! It's catchy! It makes your feet itch!"

"They won't itch much longer," said the farmer. "I'm sending him to market next Friday."

Next Friday a lorry came to the farm and drew up outside Mumpig's sty.

"What's that for, Mumpig?" asked nine of her ten spotty piglets. Henry didn't ask because he was too busy whistling.

"It's to take you to market."

"What happens there?" they said.

"Someone will buy you and fatten you up," said Mumpig.

Henry stopped whistling.

"What for?" he said.

"Never you mind," said Mumpig. "Don't bother your head about that. Just get in the lorry."

But Henry did bother his head. He did not think that this little piggy wanted to go to market. He waited until the sty door was opened and then he began to whistle the tune of the song whose words go like this:

Come follow, follow, follow,
Follow, follow, follow me.
Whither shall I follow,
follow, follow,
Whither shall I follow,
follow thee?
To the greenwood,
to the greenwood,
To the greenwood,
greenwood tree.

And he ran as fast as he could, whistling as loud as he could, past the lorry and across the farmyard and out into the fields and away to the greenwood. And after him ran his nine brothers and sisters. And after them the calves came galloping, and the lambs came gambolling, and the chicks came fluttering … all following the sound of

that one particular tune that made them feel that wherever the whistling piglet went, there they would go too.

What a business it was for the farmer and his men to catch them all again! But calves and lambs are not really happy in the depths of a wood (there's not enough grass), and nor are chicks (there are too many foxes), and at last they caught them all and took them back to the farm.

The piglets, though, were a different matter, for pigs love woods that are full of acorns and beechmast and fungi and other lovely things to eat. So it took the farmer and his men a long time to catch nine of Mumpig's ten spotty children. The tenth one they never caught. They searched the greenwood for weeks and weeks, but they saw nothing. All they heard – now and again – was the sound of someone whistling.

A Zoo in

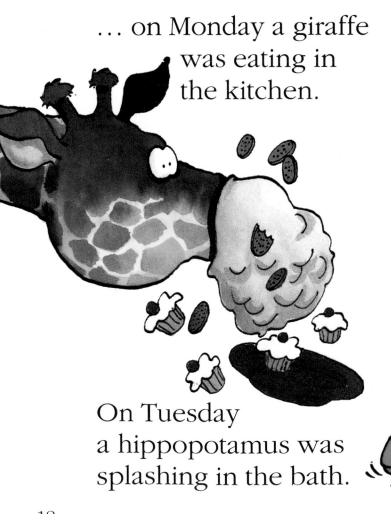

Mum and I went to
the zoo.
I said, "Can I have a zoo
in our house?"
"Certainly not," said Mum.

But …

… on Monday a giraffe
was eating in
the kitchen.

On Tuesday
a hippopotamus was
splashing in the bath.

On Wednesday a monkey
was swinging in the hall.

On Thursday
a crocodile was washing
in the garden.

Our House

by Heather Eyles
illustrated by Andy Cooke

On Friday a lion was sleeping in the living room.

On Saturday all the animals came and we had a party.

On Sunday Mum sent them all back to the zoo.

"Phew," said Mum.

But …

… she forgot the gorilla.

19

THE SNOW QUEEN

*translated by Naomi Lewis
illustrated by
Angela Barrett*

Out in the square the boldest boys would often tie their sledges to farmers' carts, and so be pulled along for quite a ride. It was enormous fun. This time, while their games were in full swing, a very large sledge arrived; it was painted white all over, and in it sat a figure muffled up in a white fur cloak and wearing a white fur hat. This sledge drove twice round the square; but, moving quickly, Kay managed to fix his own sledge behind it, and a swift ride began. The big sledge went faster and faster, then turned off into the next street. The driver looked round and nodded to Kay in the friendliest fashion, just as if they had always known each other. Every time that Kay thought of unfastening his sledge, the driver would turn and nod to him again, so he kept still. On they drove, straight out of the city gates. And now the snow began to fall so thick and fast that the little boy couldn't even see his hand in front of him as they rushed along. At last he did manage to untie the rope but it was of no use; his little sledge still clung to the big one, and they sped along like the wind. He cried out at the top of his voice, but no one heard him; the snow fell, and the sledge raced on. From time to time it seemed to jump, as if they were going over dykes and hedges. Terror seized him, he tried to say the Lord's Prayer, but all he could remember was the multiplication table.

The snowflakes grew bigger and bigger until at last they looked like great white birds. All at once they swerved to one side; the sledge came to a halt, and the driver stood up. The white fur cloak and cap were all of snow and the driver – ah, she was a lady, tall and slender, dazzlingly white! She was the Snow Queen herself.

"We've come far and fast," she said. "But you must be frozen. Creep under my bearskin cloak." She put him beside her in the sledge and wrapped the cloak around him; he felt as if he were sinking into a snowdrift. "Are you still cold?" she asked and she kissed him on the forehead. Ah-h-h! Her kiss was colder than ice; it went straight to his heart, which was already halfway to being a lump of ice. He felt as if he were dying, but only for a moment. Then he felt perfectly well, and no longer noticed the cold.

"My sledge! Don't forget my sledge!" That was the first thought that came to him. So it was tied to one of the big white birds, which flew along with the little sledge at its back. The Snow Queen kissed Kay once again, and after that he had no memory of Gerda and the grandmother, nor of anyone at home.

"Now I must give you no more kisses," said the Snow Queen, "or you will be kissed to death."

Kay looked at her. She was so beautiful; he could not imagine a wiser, lovelier face. She no longer seemed to him to be made of ice, as she once had seemed when she came to the attic window and waved to him. Now in his eyes she was perfect, and he felt no fear. He told her that he could do mental arithmetic, and fractions too; that he knew the square miles of all the principal countries, and the number of inhabitants. As he talked she smiled at him, until he began to think that what he knew was, after all, not quite so much. And he looked up into the vast expanse of the sky, as they rose up high, and she flew with him over the dark clouds, while the storm-wind whistled and raved, making him think of ballads of olden time. Over forest and lake they flew, over sea and land, beneath them screamed the icy blast; the wolves howled, the snow glittered; the black crows soared across the plains, cawing as they went. But high over all shone the great clear silver moon, and Kay gazed up at it all through the long, long winter night. During the day he slept at the Snow Queen's feet.

Little Beaver and the Echo

by Amy MacDonald
illustrated by Sarah Fox-Davies

Little Beaver lived all alone by the edge of a big pond. He didn't have any brothers. He didn't have any sisters.

Worst of all, he didn't have any friends. One day, sitting by the side of the pond, he began to cry. He cried out loud. Then he cried out louder.

Suddenly, he heard something very strange. On the other side of the pond, someone else was crying too. Little Beaver stopped crying and listened. The other crying stopped. Little Beaver was alone again.

"Booo hooo," he said.

"Booo hooo," said the voice from across the pond.

"Huh-huh-waaah!" said Little Beaver.

"Huh-huh-waaah!" said the voice from across the pond.

Little Beaver stopped crying.

"Hello!" he called.

"Hello!" said the voice from across the pond.

"Why are you crying?" asked Little Beaver.

"Why are you crying?" asked the voice from across the pond.

Little Beaver thought for a moment.

"I'm lonely," he said. "I need a friend."

"I'm lonely," said the voice from across the pond. "I need a friend."

Little Beaver couldn't believe it. On the other side of the pond lived somebody else who was sad and needed a friend.

He got right into his boat and set off to find him.

It was a big pond. He paddled and paddled. Then he saw a young duck, swimming in circles all by himself.

"I'm looking for someone who needs a friend," said Little Beaver.

"Was it you who was crying?"

"I do need a friend," said the duck.

"But it wasn't me who was crying."

"I'll be your friend," said Little Beaver. "Come with me."

So the duck jumped into the boat. They paddled and paddled. Then they saw a young otter, sliding up and down the bank all by himself.

"We're looking for someone who
  needs a friend," said Little Beaver.
"Was it you who was crying?"
"I do need a friend," said
  the otter. "But it
  wasn't me who
  was crying."
"We'll be your friends," said
  Little Beaver and the duck.
"Come with us."
  So the otter jumped into the boat.
  They paddled and paddled. Then
  they saw a young turtle, sunning
  himself all alone on a rock.
"We're looking for someone who
  needs a friend," said Little Beaver.
"Was it you who was crying?"
"I do need a friend," said the turtle.
"But it wasn't me who was crying."
"We'll be your friends," said Little
  Beaver and the duck and the otter.
"Come with us."
  So the turtle jumped into the boat,
  and they paddled and paddled until
  they came to the end of the pond.

Here lived a wise old beaver, in a
mud house, all alone. Little Beaver
told him how they had paddled all
around the pond, to find out who
was crying.
"It wasn't the duck," he said.
"It wasn't the otter. And it wasn't
  the turtle. Who was it?"
"It was the Echo," said the wise
  old beaver.
"Where does he live?" asked Little
  Beaver.
"On the other side of the pond,"
  said the wise old beaver. "No matter
  where you are, the Echo is always
  across the pond from you."
"Why is he crying?" said Little Beaver.

24

From across the pond, a voice answered him: "I have lots of friends now!"

"You see?" said the wise old beaver. "When you're happy, the Echo is happy. When you have friends, he has friends too."

"Hooray!" shouted Little Beaver and the duck and the otter and the turtle, all together. And the Echo shouted back to them: "Hooray!"

"When you are sad, the Echo is sad," said the wise old beaver. "When you are happy, the Echo is happy too."

"But how can I find him and be his friend?" asked Little Beaver.

"He doesn't have any friends, and neither do I."

"Except for me," said the duck.

"And me," said the otter.

"And me," said the turtle.

Little Beaver looked surprised.

"Yes," he said, "I have lots of friends now!" And he was so happy that he said it again, very loudly: "I have lots of friends now!"

IF I COULD WORK

If I could work
instead of play,

I'd get up early
every day.

I'd drive a bus
and shout,
"Fares, please!"

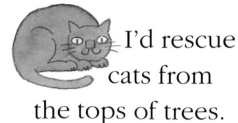I'd rescue
cats from
the tops of trees.

I'd be an inventor
and make lots
of toys,

I'd play the
guitar and make
too much noise.

I'd be the world's
favourite TV star,

I'd be a doctor
and make
children say,
"Aaaah."

I'd open a shop
with sweets on
the shelf,

When no one
was looking I'd
eat them
myself.

by Terence Blacker
illustrated by Chris Winn

I'd smile at people as they drove past, I'd stop them if they went too fast.

I'd be an incredibly silly clown, I'd make people laugh when my trousers fell down.

I'd be the first child to go to the moon, I'd tell my parents I'd be back soon. And I'd fly back home at the end of the day,

I'd really much rather work than play.

I never saw a purple cow

THERE WAS A YOUNG MAIDEN

There was a young maiden called Maggie
Whose dog was hairy and shaggy;
The front end of him was vicious and grim
But the tail end was friendly and waggy.

THERE WAS A LITTLE DOG

There was a little dog and he had a tail
And he used to wag, wag, wag it!
But when he was sad, because he'd been bad,
On the ground he would drag, drag, drag it!

Illustrated by EMMA Chichester Clark

I'VE GOT A DOG

I've got a dog as thin as a rail,
He's got fleas all over his tail;
Every time his tail goes flop,
The fleas on the bottom all hop to the top.

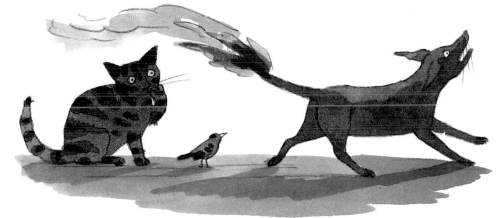

DING, DONG, DARROW

Ding, dong, darrow,
The cat and the sparrow;
The little dog has burnt his tail,
And he shall be whipped tomorrow.

An extract from # JOLLY

"My mum," said Roger to the pirates, who were all ears (well, maybe not *all* ears as some had the odd one missing), "my mum is the cleanest, tidiest person in the whole of England! And she wants me to be just like her. Every day it's the same – up before dawn, make the bed, tidy my room, get washed (here there were cries of horror from the pirates), comb my hair ("WHAT'S A COMB?"), eat my breakfast, wash the dishes, bake the bread, brush my teeth (GASP!), churn the butter, scrub the floors, iron the clothes, clean the pigsty, wash the cow, polish the goat, shampoo the chicken, whitewash the coal – on and on and on!"

(Well it was almost true thought Roger, crossing his fingers behind his back.)

"Poor wee scab!" growled the captain.

ROGER

by Colin McNaughton

"A livin' 'ell! Oooh-aargh! It ain't right fer a lad t'be brought up s'clean! By the curse of Eric the Yobbo! Tain't natural like! No, kids should be smelly and 'orrible! Tis the only chance they gits afore they grows up inter people! The on'y chance that be, oooh-aargh, unless they become pirates, ha-har! Then they can be dirty, smelly, lazy an' 'orrible all their lives! Ya-har! Curse y'all! Oooh-aargh! Ya-har!"

This fine speech by the captain was much appreciated by his crew, who cheered him and cried such things as "Yeah, that's why I joined up!" and "I'll drink t'that!" and "Down wi' soap!"

"That there mother o' yourn needs t'be taught a lesson! And we be just the chappies to be a-doin' it!" growled Abdul.

"What sez 'ee, me shoal o' sharks, eh? Should we go an' shiver 'er timbers?"

The crew replied with cries of "Aye!" and "Sounds OK to me." And so the pirates went, as pirates do, a-cursing and a-swearing, a-hooting and a-hollering, enough to give a fellow a rather nasty headache.

31

DUCK

by David Lloyd
illustrations by Charlotte Voake

 There was a time, long ago, when Tim called all animals duck.

"Duck," Tim said.

"Horse," said Granny.

"Duck," Tim said.

"Sheep," said Granny.

"Duck," Tim said.

"Speckled hen," said Granny.

So Granny took Tim to the pond.

"Duck," she said.

Tim looked and looked.

"Duck," he said.

Granny kissed him.

A little later
Tim saw a tractor.

"Truck," he said.

A little later
Tim saw a bus.

"Truck," he said.

A little later
Tim saw an old car.

"Truck," he said.

So Granny showed Tim a truck.

"Truck," she said.

Tim looked and looked.

"Truck," he said.

Granny kissed him.

For some time after this Tim never said a single word.
He just looked and looked.
He looked at his train.
He looked at his truck.
But he never said a single word.
Then Granny took Tim to the pond again.
Tim saw the duck.

He looked and looked.
The duck said, "Quack!"
"Duck," Tim said.
"Duck," Granny said.
Granny kissed Tim.
Tim kissed Granny.

All in One Piece

by Jill Murphy

Mr Large was getting ready for work. "Don't forget the office dinner-dance tonight, dear," he said. "Of course I won't," said Mrs Large. "I've been thinking about it all year."

"Are children allowed at the dinner-dance?" asked Lester.

"No," said Mrs Large. "It'll be too late for little ones."

"What about the baby?" asked Luke.

"Granny is coming to take care of everyone," said Mrs Large, "so there's no need to worry." Granny arrived at tea time. The children were already bathed and in their nightclothes. Granny gave them some painting to do while she tidied up and Mr and Mrs Large went upstairs to get ready. Luke sneaked into the bathroom while Mr Large was shaving.

"Will I have to shave when I grow up?" he asked, patting foam onto his trunk.

"Go away," said Mr Large. "I don't want you ruining my best trousers!"

The baby crept into the bedroom where Mrs Large was putting on her make-up. Mrs Large didn't notice until it was too late.

"Look!" said the baby. "Pretty!"

"Don't move," said Mrs Large. "Don't touch *anything!*"

Outside on the landing, things were even worse. Laura was clopping about in her mother's best shoes and beads and Lester and Luke were seeing how many toys they could cram into her new tights.

"Downstairs at *once!*" bellowed Mrs Large. "Can't I have just one night in the whole year to myself? One night when I am not covered in jam and poster-paint? One night when I can put on my new dress and walk through the front door all in one piece?"

The children went downstairs to Granny. Mr Large followed soon after, very smart in his best suit. At last, Mrs Large appeared in the doorway.

"How do I look?" she asked.

"Pretty, Mummy!" gasped the children.

"What a smasher!" said Mr Large.

"You look like a film star, dear," said Granny.

"Hands off!" said Mrs Large to the paint-smeared children.
Mr and Mrs Large got ready to leave.
"Goodbye everyone," they said. "Be good now."
The baby began to cry.
"Just go," said Granny, picking her up. "She'll stop as soon as you've left. Have a lovely time."

"We've escaped," said Mr Large with a smile, closing the front door behind them. "All in one piece," said Mrs Large, "and not a smear of paint between us."

"Actually," said Mr Large gallantly, "you'd look wonderful to me, even if you were *covered* in paint."

Which was perfectly true ... and just as well really!

Squelch, squelch, in the mud,

Splish, splash, scrub-a-dub,

Tickle, Tickle

by Helen Oxenbury

Gently, gently, brush your hair,
Tickle, tickle, under there.

An extract from

Melisande

by E. Nesbit

illustrated by P.J. Lynch

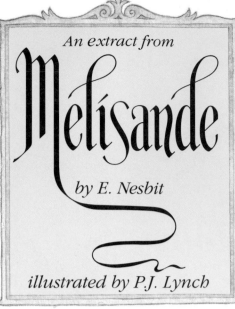

The Princess went on growing. By dinner time she was so large that she had to have her dinner brought out into the garden because she was too large to get indoors. But she was too unhappy to be able to eat anything. And she cried so much that there was quite a pool in the garden, and several pages were nearly drowned. So she remembered her *Alice in Wonderland* and stopped crying at once. But she did not stop growing. She grew bigger and bigger and bigger, till she had to go outside the palace gardens and sit on the common, and even that was too small to hold her comfortably, for every hour she grew twice as much as she had done the hour before. And nobody knew what to do, nor where the Princess was to sleep. Fortunately, her clothes had grown with her, or she would have been very cold indeed, and now she sat on the common in her green gown embroidered with gold, looking like a great hill covered with gorse in flower.

You cannot possibly imagine how large the Princess was growing, and her mother stood wringing her hands on the castle tower, and the Prince Florizel looked on broken-hearted to see his Princess snatched from his arms and turned into a lady as big as a mountain.

The King did not weep or look on. He sat down at once and wrote to his fairy godmother, asking her advice. He sent a weasel with the letter, and by return of weasel he got his own letter back again, marked, "Gone away. Left no address."

It was now, when the Kingdom was plunged into gloom, that a neighbouring King took it into his head to send an invading army against the island where Melisande lived. They came in ships and they landed in great numbers, and Melisande looking down from her height saw alien soldiers marching on the sacred soil of her country.

"I don't mind so much now," said she, "if I can really be of some use this size."

And she picked up the army of the enemy in handfuls and double handfuls, and put them back into their ships, and gave a little flip to each transport ship with her finger and thumb, which sent the ships off so fast that they never stopped till they reached their own country, and when they arrived there the whole army to a man said it would rather be court-martialled a hundred times over than go near the place again.

Meantime, Melisande, sitting on the highest hill on the island, felt the land trembling and shivering under her giant feet.

"I do believe I'm getting too heavy," she said, and jumped off the island into the sea, which was just up to her ankles. Just then a great fleet of warships and gunboats and torpedo boats came in sight, on their way to attack the island.

Melisande could easily have sunk them all with one kick, but she did not like to do this because it might have drowned the sailors, and besides, it might have swamped the island.

So she simply stooped and picked the island as you would pick a mushroom – for, of course, all islands are supported by a stalk underneath – and carried it away to another part of the world. So that when the warships got to where the island was marked on the map they found nothing but sea, and a very rough sea it was, because the Princess had churned it all up with her ankles as she walked away through it with the island.

When Melisande reached a suitable place, very sunny and warm, and with no sharks in the water, she set down the island; and the people made it fast with anchors, and then everyone went to bed, thanking the kind fate which had sent them so great a Princess to help them in their need, and calling her the saviour of her country and the bulwark of the nation.

We Love Them

by Martin Waddell
illustrated by Barbara Firth

In all the white fields there was one rabbit. It was lost. It was small. It lay in the snow.

Ben found it. Ben barked. We picked it up and took it home. Becky thought it would die, but it didn't.

It lay with Ben. Ben licked it. Becky said that Ben thought it was a little dog, and it thought Ben was a big rabbit. They didn't know they'd got it wrong. Becky said we wouldn't tell them.

We called our rabbit Zoe. She stayed with Ben. She played with Ben.

We loved them.

Zoe wasn't little for very long. She got big... and bigger... and bigger still, but not as big as Ben.

But Ben was old... and one day Ben died. We were sad and Zoe was sad. She wouldn't eat her green stuff. She sat and sat.

There was no Ben for our rabbit, until one day…in the pale hay …there was a puppy.

We took it home. It lay down with Zoe. Becky said our puppy thought Zoe was a dog. And Zoe thought our puppy

was a rabbit. They didn't know they'd got it wrong. Becky said we wouldn't tell them.

The puppy stayed. The puppy played. We loved him, just like we loved Ben.

We called our puppy Little Ben. But Little Ben got big…and bigger…and bigger

still. He got bigger than our rabbit but not as big as old Ben.

Zoe still thinks Little Ben is a rabbit, and Becky says that Zoe doesn't mind.

Becky says that Zoe likes big rabbits.

Zoe and little Ben play with us in the green fields. They arc our dog and our rabbit. We love them.

An extract from

What-a-Mess

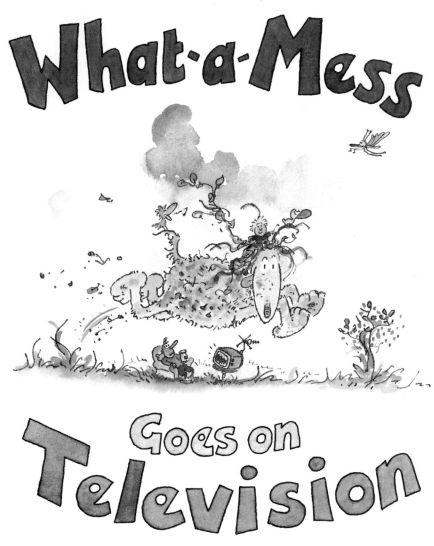

Goes on Television

by Frank Muir   *illustrated by Joseph Wright*

The story of What-a-Mess's brilliantly successful but brief (3½ minutes) television career began with the birthday party he gave for the cat-next-door. What-a-Mess had been shooed out of the house because a visitor was coming so he held the party in the garden, in his new Savoy-Ritz By-Invitation-Only No-Grown-Ups Luxury Conference and Banqueting Centre; which was an old Welsh dresser standing in the ditch with its doors missing. The shelves were narrow so space was limited and the party had to be held on three floors.

All his friends were there. What-a-Mess gave the cat-next-door the top floor all to herself (so that there would be no spitting or clawing) and she lay in state on her shelf, purring and blinking and polishing her left ear.

The middle floor was a bit of a squeeze; the Archbishop of Canterbury (now a medium-sized mongrel puppy and growing) had to share with the hedgehog, Cynthia, and both were a bit fed up when What-a-Mess took the whole of the ground floor.

But the puppy pointed out that he too was sharing. He had to make room for his new friend, Ryvita, the ladybird. (He had worked out, all by himself, that the ladybird must be a lady or it would have been called a gentlemanbird, so he christened her Ryvita. He was not sure that Ryvita was a proper girl's name but he thought it was so pretty that it *should* be even if it wasn't.)

42

44

The cat-next-door's birthday party began with a magnificent feast which What-a-Mess had prepared: cheese rinds, the paper from round a half pound of butter, an old chamois leather, a soft lump of unidentified substance found in the compost heap which might have been either a failed Coffee Fudge Angel Cake or a rotting gumboot, a plastic carton with traces of cream still in it, half a kipper, walnuts, some envelopes with plenty of glue still on them and a large piece of coal. The puppy did not know what ladybirds ate so he tempted Ryvita with a chocolate drop he was saving for himself. The ladybird flew round it, delicately landed on it as though it was a helicopter pad, folded her wings and went to sleep.

After tea, the animals chased one another at full speed through the flower beds to settle the food in their tummies. Then they sat on the grass round What-a-Mess while he told them an exciting story. It was one of the true stories his mother had told him about his famous ancestor, Sheikh Hassan of Kabul, Personal Snow-Leopard Hunter to His Majesty King Achmad XXXIV.

WHEN DAD CUTS DOWN THE CHESTNUT TREE

by

PAM AYRES

Illustrated by

GRAHAM PERCY

When Dad cuts down the chestnut
  tree,
He'll make such things for you and
  me…
A rocking horse to ride all day,
A fort where all my soldiers stay.
A little barrow painted blue,
A faithful duck on wheels for you.
Stilts to make us very tall,
Coloured bricks to build a wall.

When the tree is on the ground,
All my friends will come around.
On the trunk we'll jump and climb,
We will have a lovely time!
No more tearing jacket sleeves,
No more sweeping up of leaves.
And when I'm tucked into my bed,
Kisses kissed and goodnights said,
The tree won't scare me any more,
When the night wind makes it roar.
If there wasn't any tree
What difference would it make to me?
No tree-house – that's the worst of all –
To hide in when we hear Mum call.
No cool places in the shade,
When we have run and jumped and
    played.
No leaves to kick and throw about
And roll each other in and shout.
No sticks to find on chilly days,
To make our winter fires blaze

And there is another thing –
What will happen to our swing?
Where will owl and squirrel stay
If the tree is hauled away?
If the tree is really gone,
What can I hang my nestbox on?
Suddenly we're not so sure
We want it cut down any more.
Trees are special, large or small,
So Dad – don't cut it down *at all!*

Dad was so tired the next day that he didn't get up early. Mum took him a cup of tea in bed. While the rest of the family were having breakfast, they heard a great noise in the street. They all hurried outside. A lorry had arrived at their house.

It was huge! It had a big drum that turned slowly round and round – CRRURK, CRRURK, CRRURK! On the side of the lorry was written "JIFFY READY-MIX CONCRETE CO".

Out jumped jolly Joe Best. "Load of concrete you ordered!" he called cheerfully. "Not this morning, surely?" said Mum. "I'm sure we didn't..." But it was too late. Jimmy had already pulled a lever and the big drum poured out a load of concrete, all in a rush.

Slop! Slurp! Dollop! Splosh! Just like that! It landed in a shivering heap right outside the Pattersons' front door. Dad rushed downstairs, pulling on his trousers over his pyjamas. "We weren't expecting you today!" he shouted. "That's OK. Just sign here," said Joe. Then he leapt back into his seat. "It's quick-setting!" he called from the cab window. "Be hard as a rock in a couple of hours. Better get busy!" "But we haven't..." Dad called back. But Jimmy was already revving up the engine. The big concrete lorry roared away up the street in a cloud of dust. "Quick!" cried Dad, picking up a shovel. "Quick!" shrieked Mum, searching for a spade.

Concrete Lorry *by Shirley Hughes*

"Grab those buckets!"
"Fetch the
  wheelbarrow!"
"Run for the
  neighbours!"
*"The quick-
setting concrete
is soon going to set!"*
Never had the Pattersons moved so
fast. Mum began to shovel up the
concrete into the wheelbarrow and
trundle it through the house, while
Dad shovelled and smoothed it down
over the foundation at the back.
Josie and Harvey ran to fetch Mr Lal
and Rhajit from next
door and Frankie
and Mae's dad from
up the street.
And they all
came running.
The neighbours
pitched in and
shovelled and
spread too. Josie,
Harvey and
little Pete ran up and down with
buckets. Murdoch joined in,
barking loudly.

Everyone laboured and
  struggled and fell
  over one another's
  feet. They
  shovelled
  and heaved
  and trundled
concrete from the front of the house to
the back. And steadily the heap on
the pavement grew smaller
and smaller.
"Quick! It's
beginning to set!"
shouted Mum.
Everybody
worked faster
and faster.
"Done at last!"
gasped Dad, throwing down his shovel
  and wiping his hands on his
  trousers. Then all the
  workers rested. The
  foundation
  was finished. Only a
  small hill of concrete
  was left beside the front
  door. It had set so hard
  that nothing in the world
  would shift it.

Our Dog

by Helen Oxenbury

Our dog has to go for a
walk every day. She stares
at us until we take her.

One day she found
a smelly pond and
jumped into it.

"Poo! You smell
disgusting!" we told her.
Then she rolled in the mud.
"Pretend she's not ours," whispered
Mum. "We must get her home
quickly and give her a bath."

50

We made her wait outside
the kitchen door.
Mum filled the bath.
"I'll put her in," Mum said.
"Now hold on tight! Don't let her jump out."

"Quick! Where's the towel?"
Mum shouted. "She'll make
everything wet!"

We chased her
out of the kitchen and
down the hall.

She ran up the stairs
and into the bedroom.
We caught her
on the bed.

"It's no good!" Mum said.
"We'll just have to take her
for another walk, to dry
in the air."

53

On Saturday night I lost my wife,
And where do you think I found her?
Up in the moon, singing a tune,
And all the stars around her.

Sally go round the sun,
Sally go round the moon,
Sally go round the chimney-pots
On a Saturday afternoon.

54

Moon

illustrated by *Charlotte Voake*

Hey diddle, diddle,

The cat and the fiddle,

The cow jumped over the moon.

The little dog laughed

To see such sport,

And the dish ran away with the spoon.

The man in the moon

Came tumbling down,

And asked his way to Norwich.

He went by the south,

And burnt his mouth

With supping cold pease-porridge.

Beep beep! Here come...

THE HORRIBLES

SLOB HEAD

FRECKLE BELLY

BONE BUM

FAT FOOT

a story from *The Horribles* by

Michael Rosen

HORRIBLE BABY

illustrated by

John Watson

Horrible Baby was
in its cot, gurgling. The other
Horribles – Slob Head, Fat
Foot, Freckle Belly and Bone
Bum – were having breakfast.
They were eating dollops.
There was a big pile of them
in the middle of the table.
Every now and then one of
the Horribles grabbed a
dollop and stuffed it into its
mouth. But sometimes
another Horrible tried to
grab it first.

Fat Foot had a dollop in each
hand. Slob Head grabbed one
of Fat Foot's dollops, so Fat
Foot wheeled round and
slopped the other dollop into
Slob Head's face.

This was breakfast time with
the Horribles.

"I'm worried about Horrible
Baby," said Slob Head. "It's
not horrible enough."

"Oh, I think Horrible Baby is
plenty horrible enough," said
Fat Foot.

"Rubbish!" said Slob Head.

"Listen to it."

The Horribles went quiet
and listened.

Horrible Baby was going,
"Ooofle, ooofle, ooofle!"

"Do you hear that?" said Slob
Head. "It's too nice, much too
nice."

Freckle Belly looked up from
its dollop.

"We could teach Horrible Baby
some horrible noises," said
Freckle Belly.

"Yes," said Bone Bum, "like
schmarfle and *erg durg
nabber.*"

"Good," said Slob Head. "Very
good."

"I'll go and get Horrible Baby,"
said Bone Bum.

This was Bone Bum's
favourite job.

It crept very slowly up to
Horrible Baby's door and then
with a great rush it pushed
the door open and roared,
"GRUNKLE GRUNKLE
GRUNKLE GRUNKLE
GRUNKLE!!!!!!!!!!!"

Horrible Baby looked at Bone
Bum and smiled. "Bone Bum
silly!" said Horrible Baby.

"No, Bone Bum really scary,"
roared Bone Bum, and
then Bone Bum put its
nose into its mouth, waved
its arms in the air and roared,

"UNGER UNGER UNGER
UNGER UNGER UNGER!!!!!!!!"
– which was meant to be
grunkle grunkle grunkle, but
unger unger unger was all
Bone Bum could manage
with its nose in its mouth.
Horrible Baby loved it.
It wasn't scared at all.

"Come on then," said Bone
Bum, feeling a little fed up.

"Come and have your
dollops."

So Horrible Baby got up and
joined the other Horribles for
breakfast.

"Don't want dollops!" said
Horrible Baby. "Want my
bottle! Want my bottle! Want
my bottle!"

"No," said Fat Foot. "You must
have your dollops."

Horrible Baby started to
scream. "WANT MY BOTTLE
WANT MY BOTTLE WANT
MY BOTTLE WANT
MY BOTTLE!!!!!!!"

57

Slob Head put its hands over its ears, which was very difficult because Slob Head's hands were very small and its ears were enormous.

"Oh, stop the noise! Stop the noise!" said Slob Head.

"You must have your dollops," said Fat Foot, "and then you'll grow up to be a great big Horrible."

"WANT MY BOTTLE WANT MY BOTTLE WANT MY BOTTLE!" Horrible Baby went on screaming.

Freckle Belly got up and put some watery mud in Horrible Baby's bottle. Horrible Baby grabbed it. Slob Head took its hands off its ears and watched. As Horrible Baby sucked on its bottle, there were great long bubbly sucky noises.

Sklersh frernch! Sklersh frernch! Sklush frunch! Sklush frunch! Sklish frinch! Sklish frinch! Slob Head quickly put its hands over its ears again.

"Oh the noise, the noise, I can't stand it!" Fat Foot said.

"Listen, Horrible Baby, that's a really nasty noise, not the sort of noise we want to hear from you at all."

Freckle Belly giggled. Secretly, Freckle Belly really wanted to make Horrible Baby bottle-sucking noises itself.

"It's not funny," said Slob Head. "That noise is disgusting. You could help by teaching it some proper Horrible Noises."

"All right," said Freckle Belly. "Come on, Bone Bum, come and help."

So Bone Bum and Freckle Belly took Horrible Baby into Horrible Baby's room and started to teach it Horrible Noises.

"Listen here, Horrible Baby," said Bone Bum. "When you grow up you're going to be horrible, OK? That means when you go out, you've got to be really horrible wherever you go. You might be in the street or somewhere and so you've got to learn to scream horrible noises and scare people, OK?"

"Like this," said Freckle Belly.

Freckle Belly lifted its arms in the air and started shaking all over. Then it roared, "Slob slob slob gluck nucker! Slob slob slob gluck nucker!"

"Now you try," said Bone Bum.

Horrible Baby looked at the two Horribles for a moment and very slowly pulled the bottle out of its mouth. There was just one more moment and then the watery mud that was supposed to be in Horrible Baby's tummy started gurgling up out of its mouth.

"Blurk blurk blurk!" said Horrible Baby, as the watery mud slithered out of its mouth and down its chin.

"Oh no!" said Freckle Belly, turning away. "That's awful!"

"Oh no no no no no!" said Bone Bum, and began to run away.

"Slob Head, quick, come here!" said Freckle Belly. "Horrible Baby is being terrible!"

In came Slob Head and Fat Foot.

"Now that's really naughty," said Fat Foot. "Just look at the mess."

"I can't bear to look at it," said Freckle Belly.

"Nor me," said Bone Bum.

"Wait a minute," said Slob Head. "I've just thought of something. Why did you go in there with Horrible Baby?"

"To teach it horrible noises, of course," said Freckle Belly.

"Well, what's the matter then?" said Slob Head.

"Well," said Bone Bum. "Horrible Baby's being naughty. It won't learn the horrible words. Instead it keeps being… er… er… er…"

"It keeps being what?" said Slob Head.

"It keeps being horrible," said Bone Bum.

"Well, there you are then," said Slob Head. "Horrible Baby is being horrible."

"I don't like it," said Freckle Belly.

"I do," said Slob Head.

"Blurk blurk blurk!" said Horrible Baby.

THE YELLOW HOUSE

BY
**BLAKE
MORRISON**

⋅⋙⋘⋅

ILLUSTRATED BY
**HELEN
CRAIG**

Every day we passed the yellow house on our way to the park, Mum and me and my little sister Jenny. The house was on its own. It looked old, sad and rather scary.

At the little wooden gate Mum would lift me up to show me the garden. There was a lawn, a goldfish pond, a greenhouse, an apple tree, a dustbin, a garden gnome. But never any people, never any children.

One day Jenny dropped her teddy near the yellow house and Mum went back to fetch it. I climbed the wooden gate all by myself. Inside the garden was a boy in dungarees and a bobble hat. He waved to me.

**"Come inside!"
he shouted.
"Come and play with me."**

I pulled myself over and slid my legs down till they touched the pebbly path. The garden looked huge. The boy stood on the lawn.

**"Come and see this!"
he shouted.
"Come and see this."**

I ran and looked. In the long grass a tiger was playing with its cubs. They cuffed and scratched each other. They growled at me.

But the boy had moved off to the goldfish pond.

**"Come and see this!"
he shouted.
"Come and see this."**

I ran and looked. A white dolphin swam out from the lily pads, leapt in the air and splashed down on the water. It wiggled its tail at me. But the boy had gone inside the greenhouse.

**"Come and see this!"
he shouted.
"Come and see this."**

I ran and looked. A green snake was winding its body round the cane of a tomato plant. It shimmied and hissed.

It stuck out its tongue at me. But the boy was standing under the apple tree.

"Come and see this!" he shouted. "Come and see this."

I ran and looked. A pelican was roosting on a branch. It swallowed an apple with a *chomp chomp*. It wobbled its pouch at me.

But the boy had opened the dustbin.

"Come and see this!" he shouted. "Come and see this."

I ran and looked. Inside the dustbin a panda was reading a newspaper. It squinted and ho-hoed. It lifted its hat when it saw me.

But the boy was striding through the front door of the house.

"Come and see this!" he shouted. "Come and see this."

I ran to look but the boy had closed the door. I stretched and stretched, right up on my tiptoes, but the handle was too high for me.

I rang the bell but no one came to answer.

Now Mum had seen me and was calling from the wooden gate. She looked cross. I walked very slowly down the pebbly path. Mum lifted me back over the gate. "Where have you been?" she asked. "Jenny was worried."

Then Mum gave me a great big kiss.

We still go past the yellow house on our way to the park, Mum and me and my little sister Jenny. Mum lifts me up to see the garden. There is a lawn, a goldfish pond, a greenhouse, an apple tree, a dustbin, a garden gnome. Never any people though, never any children, never the boy who waved to me. But I know one day he'll be there again calling me in to play.

Beaky

by Jez Alborough

An egg tumbled down through the leaves and branches and shattered into pieces on the rain forest floor.

Out popped a fluffy creature with a bright blue beak and a curly orange tail.

"Hello," croaked Frog, jumping out from behind a bush.

"I'm a frog, what are you?" The creature looked confused.

"Don't you know what you are?" asked Frog. The creature shook its head.

"Then you can be my friend," said Frog.

"I will call you Beaky. Come on, let's go for a walk."

"Am I a frog?" asked Beaky as they hopped along. Frog laughed.

"If you were a frog," he said, "then you would be able to hop as high as me and you wouldn't have those funny fluffy flaps."

"If I'm not a frog," said Beaky, "then what am I?"

"I don't know," puzzled Frog, "I've never seen anything like you before; but you must be something…everything is something!"

Before long they found Snake. "What's he doing?" asked Beaky. "Slithering," said Frog. "Precisely," said Snake. "It's simply splendid to slither, you should try a slither yourself."

62

"Yes, have a try," said Frog, for he wondered whether Beaky might be some sort of snake. So Beaky lay on the earth and tried to slither. Nothing happened.

"Oh dear," said Frog. Snake laughed. "Too short," he said, and slithered off into the trees. Beaky and Frog hopped to the river where they found Fish gliding about in the water.

"What's he doing?" asked Beaky.

"I'm swimming," said Fish. "Come and join me, the water's lovely."

"Good idea," said Frog, thinking that Beaky might be some sort of fish. "Try a swim."

Beaky splished and splashed and flipped and flapped, but couldn't swim a stroke. "Oh dear," said Frog. Fish giggled. "Too fluffy," he said, and swam away.

"Everyone knows what they are except me," sighed Beaky. Just then he heard something singing softly, far away.

"Did you hear that?" he said excitedly. "Hear what?" said Frog.

"Listen!" said Beaky. "It came from up there." Frog looked up to the top of the trees, then he heard it too.

"Someone up there must be really happy," said Beaky, "to sing such a joyful song. Do you think I could ever be that happy?"

"Maybe," said Frog, "but not until we discover what you are." Then he had an idea.

"Let's climb up there," he said, "and see if we can find out." So up they went, but the higher they climbed the more frightened Frog became. So Beaky had to go on alone. On and on he struggled, all through the day and into the night until he could go no further.

"Now I'm lost," cried Beaky, "and I still haven't found out what I am. Maybe I should never have left the forest floor. Perhaps the song was just a dream." And with this thought, he slept. Beaky awoke the next morning to the sound of a familiar song. Looking round, he saw circling in the air a beautiful fluffy creature with a bright blue beak and a curly orange tail.

"What are you?" called Beaky.

"I'm a bird," sang the creature, "a bird of Paradise."

"A bird," said Beaky, "that's what I am."

In his excitement he jumped and skipped and dipped, he strutted, bobbed and trotted and then...

he tripped!

Down and down he fell, crashing through leaves and branches, down towards the earth below.

"Flap your wings!" called the bird. "Flap your wings!" Beaky opened wide his fluffy flaps. "My wings," he cried, "these are my *wings*." And with a *whoosh* he began to fly...up past a tree where Snake was slithering...down to the river where Fish was swimming...and back to the vine where Frog was still waiting.

"Frog," said Beaky, "look at me. I can't slither, or swim, or hop like you, but I can *fly!*"

At that moment Beaky heard the singing once more and it seemed to be calling him.

"I must go," he said, "but I'll come back and visit." Then he flew up towards the treetops.

"Beaky," called Frog, "you haven't told me what you are."

"I'm a bird," cried Beaky. "I'm a bird…a bird of Paradise!"

An extract from
EDMOND WENT

Edmond had been so excited by the sight of his new country that he had run a few steps down the other side of the hill. Now he found he could no longer see the copse, his fields, the barn or the farmhouse. He ran quickly back onto the top of the hill, looked back the way he had come.

There was the farmhouse; he could see his bedroom window and just make out

one of his yellow curtains which had been caught by the wind and was now lazily flapping in the breeze. Edmond turned the other way and looked at his new world; he was on a boundary between the Old World and the New. He hesitated for a moment, wondering which way to go. Then his eye caught a movement

quite close to him. A familiar figure was walking up the path towards him. It was his father.

Edmond gave him a half wave and turned into the New World. He walked down to the lake where the rushes grew. The ground got very boggy but there were tussocks you could stand on safely. Edmond pulled at the reeds; they were firmly rooted but finally he got up a good long one which he held up in front of him like a sword as he walked on round the lake.

Where the boat was moored, Edmond found the bank was propped up by some wooden boards which had been driven into the water. This meant you could walk right up to the edge of the lake. Lying down, he could lean over the edge then just get his hand into the water and make some satisfactory waves which rocked the boat.

Edmond got up, pulled on the rope that moored the boat and, when it was against the bank, jumped in. In the boat were oars, but they were too big for

FAR AWAY

by Martin Bax
illustrated by Michael Foreman

Edmond to use although he could just lift them. Just then Edmond's father came up. He put down a big bundle he was carrying, untied the rope that moored the boat and stepping down into it pushed them out into the lake.

Edmond was surprised to see how well his father rowed. They rowed out to the centre of the lake because Edmond wished to speak to the swan. But the swan swam away from them in a circle. They rowed after it, but it kept circling. They tried to row straight towards it. It looked at them, but bowed its head twice at them, quite politely, and then swam away.

They moored the boat again and Edmond walked round the lake, picking up wood that had collected at the edge. In his bundle, Edmond's father had a frying pan and some sausages. They built a fire with the driftwood and ate sausages, baked beans and filled up with bags of crisps. By now it was quite dark

and the moon had come up. Edmond was glad to find that his father had brought him his sleeping bag. They had built their fire a little up the hill from the lake. Edmond could snuggle down and look out over the water. Wreaths of mist spiralled up from the lake. They looked, Edmond thought, like ghostly people, but friendly because they came from his lake. As they grew bigger he saw that they had the faces of all the people he liked best. All the people he had left at home when he had come far away.

NONSENSE RHYMES

Gregory Griggs,
Gregory Griggs,
Had twenty-seven different wigs.
He wore them up,
He wore them down,
To please the people of the town;
He wore them east,
He wore them west;
But he never could tell
Which he liked best.

Old Mother Shuttle
Lived in a coal-scuttle,
Along with her dog and her cat;
What they ate I can't tell,
But 'tis known very well,
That not one of the party was fat.

Old Mother Shuttle
Scoured out her coal-scuttle,
And washed both her dog and her cat;
The cat scratched her nose,
So they came to hard blows
And who was the gainer by that?

illustrated by Nicola Bayley

I dreamed a dream next Tuesday week,
Beneath the apple trees;
I thought my eyes were big pork pies,
And my nose was Stilton cheese.
The clock struck twenty minutes to six,
When a frog sat on my knee;
I asked him to lend me eighteen pence,
But he borrowed a shilling of me.

There was an old lady of Wales,
Who lived upon oysters and snails.
Upon growing a shell,
She exclaimed, "It is well,
I won't have to wear bonnets or veils."

MRS GOOSE'S

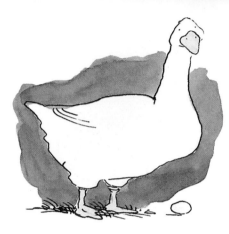

One day Mrs Goose found an egg and made a lovely nest to put it in. Mrs Goose sat on the egg to keep it safe and warm. Soon the egg started

to crack open. The little bird inside was pecking at the shell. Mrs Goose's baby was very very small and fluffy and yellow.

Mrs Goose took her baby out to eat some grass. But her baby didn't want to eat grass. She ran off to look for something different.

Mrs Goose took her naughty baby to the pond.

The water looked cold and grey.

Poor Mrs Goose! Her baby would not swim!

BABY

by Charlotte Voake

The baby grew and grew and grew.

Mrs Goose's feathers were smooth and white.

Mrs Goose's baby had untidy brown feathers.

Mrs Goose had large webbed feet.

Her baby had little pointed toes.

The baby followed Mrs

Goose everywhere,

and cuddled up to her at night.

Mrs Goose guarded her

baby from strangers.

Mrs Goose's baby never did eat much grass.

The baby never did go swimming in the pond.

And everyone except Mrs Goose knew why.

Mrs Goose's baby was a
CHICKEN!

A House in Town

by William Mayne
illustrated by
Sarah Fox-Davies

Foxy mother Vixen lives in the town. One night she stalks her prey along the hills high above the houses.

Another night she forages from bins and heaps beside the shops and houses of the town.

This night she crossed the river to hunt in woods still wild.

"I see her late at night and early in the day," the bridge-keeper tells his friends. "She does not need to pay to pass."

This night is turning into day when Vixen comes to her children hidden in the town, beneath a house in a sloping street: Rack, and Rennie, and little Ryll. By day they sleep. By night they watch the door and wait. In and out come shadows, Fox, their father, Vixen mother.

The night is turning into day when she rounds without a sound the last street corner.

There, instead of empty street and stillness, is a gang of men. Vixen crouches on a wall to see and hear. The men are at her house with large machines like birds, tall and beaked, pecking, eating, at her home.

Vixen listens for her husband Fox. She hears machines; she smells falling dust; she sees breaking house; she feels awful fear.

She runs under wheels, among feet, between falling stones. She creeps to the door and jumps. No man sees her.

Rack and Rennie and little Ryll are already wakened, terrified. There is no sign of Fox, their father, who is hunting far and wide tonight.

Vixen has to do the best she can alone. She knows what it must be. Little Ryll she carries, because she cannot walk. Rack and Rennie follow.

"Stay close," says Vixen. "We'll run like one; they will not see us pass."

They come into the gardens of a city square. Rack and Rennie love the day and want to run about. Little Ryll has tried and cannot tumble very far.

"We must go," says Vixen. She sees an empty street. It leads upwards, a weary way to the hills and another home.

That street, and yet another street, they walk. Their tongues hang out. They creep from gate to gate; they crawl from tree to tree; they slink through garden hedge and fence.

Rack grows tired; Rennie lags behind. Vixen goes ahead.

In front of Rack and Rennie walks a terrier dog. He does not see them, though they see him and know of danger in their hearts. He sees Vixen with little Ryll.

His hackles rise. He calls out. He knows that Vixen is a fox. He calls again for other dogs to help, and begins the hunt. He has dreamed of chase and this is it.

Vixen looks back for Rack and Rennie. They are not close. All she can do is run.

Rack and Rennie look at each other, frightened now. They lie low and wait. What to do they cannot tell: they have not learned to live or stay alive.

Vixen goes on up the hill. Towards her run two spotted dogs. From an alley runs a fattish beagle out of breath, and its master just the same.

Vixen cannot go on up the hill. She turns aside. She knows all the city ways. A playful puppy thinks it will win at once and tips Vixen over in the road.

Vixen drops poor Ryll and bites the pup. But spotted dogs are upon her, beagle, terrier, and more. When they've gone, and Vixen too, Ryll is sitting all alone and whimpering.

Rack and Rennie run to her. Rack picks her up. Rennie sniffs the ground. "This way," she says, and sets off down the hill, where Vixen went before.

They follow on. Where Vixen ran the scent is clear for them. It is clear too for dogs, and they begin to come behind. The way is very hard, where Vixen scrambled up a wall, along the top, and down a dizzy gate; or squeezed through a narrow drain. Dogs come out of all the houses.

Rack has to stop. He has no breath. He puts Ryll down and Rennie carries her. They run on again, but very slow, though down the hill.

A strange thing happens now behind them. The chasing dogs run off to the right, along a different street. The reason is soon clear. Padding fast and gentle there comes Fox their father. "Go on," he says, "your mother's making for the bridge. I'll cross your track and cross your trail, and draw the pack away. But hurry on and do not wait for me," he calls, and swiftly goes.

Hurry on they do, by factories and railways, where Vixen's scent is leading them.

All the time the dogs are calling in the streets behind. Ahead of Rack and Rennie sirens sound where police cars clear the road for them. Foxes cannot know of that, or how men come on the

street to see them pass by day. The little foxes only know that they must run.

At a cross-roads all the traffic lights are red. In the middle Vixen waits, not knowing whether the cubs are safe.

Rennie drops young Ryll. Vixen gives all three a lick, tells them they must hurry yet; and leads the way. The traffic waits and watches. It seems that men can do no more to help, nor stop the pack of dogs.

The dogs run wildly down the hill, all noise. In front, and turning now and then to tease, is Fox, loping just ahead.

Vixen is on the bridge. The wild wood lies beyond. Out of breath beside her Rack and Rennie walk. In her jaws is Ryll. No man or truck, car or bus, is with them now.

They cross the river. Men begin to clap their hands, pleased at the escape.

"It does not help," says Vixen. "We are not safe. Dogs are coming too." She looks back. But when she does she sees a gap begin to open in the road, where the keeper lifts the bridge so no dog can cross that place. He does not know that Fox is still to follow.

The dogs come on and on. Fox is tired now, his ears more flat. Vixen's heart stands still in pain; men clap their hands no more:

they did not know of Fox and see no escape for him. Fox runs on the bridge, up the lifting road to the gap, and looks at it. He sits there calm. The dogs run up to him, and when they do he rises to his toes and jumps, clear across the gap and to the other side. "Good day, gentlemen," he says to them, and turns away to smile at Vixen and the cubs.

Crawling, yelping dogs fall off the bridge, through the gap and into water, over the edge and into mud. Some swim up the docks, others muddle back to land; none cross the river.

Now Fox is safe men clap again, and cheer. Vixen's heart begins to beat once more.

Fox licks her nose for love. The family, together now and safe, hurry under the trees.

The keeper of the bridge has his picture in the paper for kindness to creatures of the wood still wild.

An extract from

Judy the Bad Fairy

by Martin Waddell
illustrated by
Dom Mansell

PUFF!
PanT!
Phew!

The Fairy Queen had a Good Long Think, and then she snapped her fingers and said, "T E E T H !"
"Teeth?" said Judy, halfway to the hammock.
"I'm putting you on teeth!" the Fairy Queen snapped. "You can be Tooth Fairy for the Realm. There's your Toothbag, and there's your Under-the-Pillow Money. Bring back at least fourteen teeth each night at midnight, OR ELSE!"
Fourteen teeth is a lot of teeth.
Poor Judy had to scoot about.
Most of the poor people had no teeth, or very black ones, so by and large she stuck to the Castle. Most of the people in the castle had bedrooms at the top of the tall towers. Upstairs and downstairs ran Judy top speed, teeth-gathering and money-under-pillow dumping.
"I've fixed her this time!" said the Fairy Queen delightedly. And all the Good Fairies held a Fairy Party in the Dell to celebrate, and took turns in Judy's honeysuckle hammock.
Judy got so tired that her Fairy Legs wouldn't work any more. She sank down halfway up the tallest tower, and lay there like a dead Fairy. Then...

SNORE! SNORE!
SNORE! SNORE!

The Snoring was coming
from behind a door. Judy
opened it, looking for
somewhere to lie down.
And…it was the King's
Aunty Chamber! All the
King's Aunties were
asleep there.

Each one had a little bed all to herself, and
beside each little bed there was a little
table, and on each little table there was a
little glass, and in each little glass was…
a set of T E E T H !
Judy nabbed the nearest.
There were twenty-eight teeth in it, which
meant Judy was able to take the weekend
off in the
honeysuckle
hammock,
and still hand
in fourteen
teeth each
night at the
stroke of twelve.

WHERE'S WALLY? THE ULTIMATE FUN BOOK!
OH WHAT A LOVELY MAZE!

WOW, WALLY-WATCHERS, DO YOU REMEMBER THIS AMAZING MAZE, WHERE WE ALL GOT LOST IN THE ULTIMATE FUN BOOK? PHEW, FANTASTIC, IT'S TRULY ASTONISHING! CAN YOU FIND YOUR WAY THROUGH THE MAZE? CAN YOU FIND ME? CAN YOU FIND WILMA? CAN YOU FIND WOOF? CAN YOU FIND THE ONE PERSON HERE WHO HAS NO HAT OR HOOD ON? CAN YOU FIND MY LOST KEY? CAN YOU FIND TEN LOST GLOVES? WOW, I TELL YOU, THE CLOSER YOU LOOK, THE MORE YOU FIND! BE MERRY, WALLY-WATCHERS,
    BE MERRY, FOR HAPPINESS IS LIFE!

Wally

Wally

Wilma

Woof

Eat Up, Gemma

by Sarah Hayes
illustrated by
Jan Ormerod

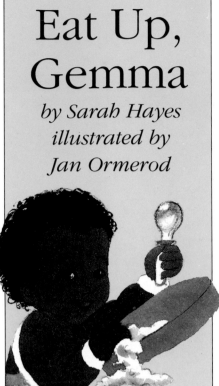

One morning we woke up late. I couldn't find my shoes and Gemma wouldn't eat her breakfast.
"Eat up, Gemma," said Mum, but Gemma threw her breakfast on the floor. Later on we went to the market. Mum bought a bag of apples and some bananas. The man at the fruit stall gave me a bunch of grapes. He gave some to Gemma too.
"Eat up, Gemma," said the man, but Gemma pulled the grapes off one by one and squashed them.

When we got home Grandma had made the dinner.
"Nice and spicy," Dad said, "just how I like it."
It was nice and spicy all right. I drank three glasses of water.
"Eat up, Gemma," said Grandma.
Gemma banged her spoon on the table and shouted. But she didn't eat a thing. The next day was Saturday and Dad took us to the park. We had chocolate biscuits for a treat. I ate two and then another two.
"Eat up, Gemma," said Dad. But Gemma didn't eat her biscuit. She just licked off all the chocolate and gave the rest to the birds.

In the evening our friends were having a party.
"Eat up, everyone," said our friends. And we did, all except Gemma. She sat on Grandma's knee and gave her dinner to the dog when Grandma wasn't looking.

After the party my friend came to stay and we had a midnight feast. Gemma didn't have any. She was too tired.
In the morning we made Gemma a feast.
"Eat up, Gemma," said my friend. Gemma picked up her toy hammer and banged her feast to pieces. My friend thought it was funny, but Mum and Dad didn't.

Soon it was time for us to put on our best clothes and go to church. I sang very loudly. The lady in front of us had a hat with fruit on it. I could see Gemma looking and looking.

When everyone was really quiet Gemma leaned forward. "Eat up, Gemma," she said.

Then she tried to pull a grape off the lady's hat. She pulled and pulled and the lady's hat fell off. Gemma hid her face in Dad's coat.

"Eat up, Gemma," I said. And she did. She ate all the grapes and the bananas. She even tried to eat the skins.

"Thank goodness for that," said Mum.

"We were getting worried," said Dad.

Grandma smiled at me. I felt very proud.

"Gemma eat up," said Gemma, and we all laughed.

When we got home I had an idea. I found a plate and a bowl. I turned the bowl upside down and put it on the plate. Then I took a bunch of grapes and two bananas and put them on the plate. It looked just like the lady's hat.

LITTLE RABBIT FOO FOO

retold by
Michael Rosen

illustrated by
Arthur Robins

Little Rabbit Foo Foo riding through the forest, scooping up the field mice and bopping them on the head.

Down came the Good Fairy and

said, "Little Rabbit Foo Foo, I don't like your attitude, scooping up the field mice and bopping them on the head. I'm going to give you three chances to change, and if you don't, I'm going to turn you into a **goonie**."

Little Rabbit Foo Foo riding through the forest, scooping up the wriggly worms and bopping them on the head.

Down came the Good Fairy and said, "Little Rabbit Foo Foo, I don't like your attitude, scooping up the wriggly

82

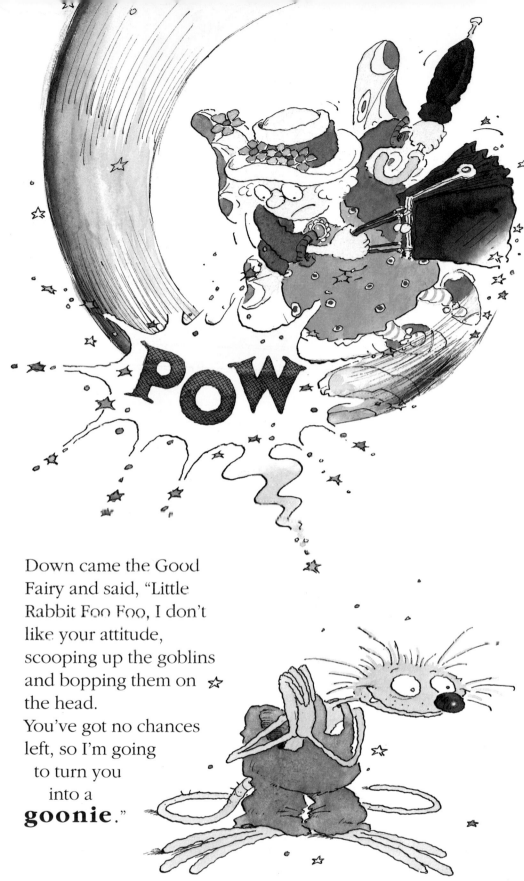

worms and bopping them on the head. You've got two chances to change, and if you don't, I'm going to turn you into a **goonie**."

Little Rabbit Foo Foo riding through the forest, scooping up the tigers and bopping them on the head.

Down came the Good Fairy and said, "Little Rabbit Foo Foo, I don't like your attitude, scooping up the tigers and bopping them on the head. You've got one chance left to change, and if you don't, I'm going to turn you into a **goonie**."

Little Rabbit Foo Foo riding through the forest, scooping up the goblins and bopping them on the head.

Down came the Good Fairy and said, "Little Rabbit Foo Foo, I don't like your attitude, scooping up the goblins and bopping them on the head. You've got no chances left, so I'm going to turn you into a **goonie**."

83

Sally and the Limpet

by Simon James

Not long ago, on a Sunday, Sally was down on the beach exploring, when she found a brightly coloured, bigger-than-usual limpet shell. She wanted to take it home but, as she pulled, the limpet made a little squelching noise and held on to the rock. The harder Sally tugged, the more tightly the limpet held on, until, suddenly, Sally slipped and fell – with the limpet stuck to her finger.

Though she pulled with all her might, it just wouldn't come off. So she ran over to her dad. He heaved and groaned, but the limpet made a little squelching noise and held on even tighter.

So, that afternoon, Sally went home in the car with a limpet stuck to her finger. When they got home, her dad tried using his tools.

Her brother tried offering it lettuce and cucumber.

But, that night, Sally went to bed with a limpet stuck to her finger.

Next day it was school. All her friends tried to pull the limpet off her finger.

84

Mr Wobblyman, the nature teacher, said that limpets live for twenty years, and stay all their lives on the same rock.

In the afternoon, Sally's mother took her to the hospital, to see the doctor. He tried chemicals, injections, potions and pinchers.

Sally was beginning to feel upset. Everyone was making too much fuss all around her. She kicked over the doctor's chair and ran. She ran through the endless corridors. She just wanted to be on her own. She ran out of the hospital and through the town. She didn't stop when she got to the beach. She ran through people's sandcastles. She even ran over a fat man.

When she reached the water, she jumped in with all her clothes on. Sally landed with a big splash and then just sat in the water.

The limpet, feeling at home once more, made a little squelching noise and wiggled off her finger.

But Sally didn't forget what Mr Wobblyman, the nature teacher, had said. Very carefully, she lifted the limpet by the top of its shell. She carried it back across the beach, past the fat man she had walked on, and gently, so gently, she put the limpet back on the very same rock where she had found it the day before.

Then, humming to herself, she took the long way home across the beach.

an extract from Pog

Pog painted

by Peter Haswell

Pog painted the ceiling red.

He painted the wall red.

He painted the floor red.

He painted the fireplace red.

Pog painted the chair red.

He painted his boots red.

He painted his feet red.

Pog said, "I don't know

why I did all that …"

"I don't much like red!"

The Grumpalump

by Sarah Hayes
illustrated by Barbara Firth

The bear stared at
the grumpalump.
The lump grumped.

The bear stared and the
cat sat on the grumpalump.
The lump grumped.

The bear stared, the cat sat
and the mole rolled
   on the grumpalump.
      The lump grumped.

The bear stared, the cat sat,
the mole rolled and the dove
shoved the grumpalump.
The lump still grumped.

The bear stared, the cat sat,
the mole rolled, the dove
shoved and the bull
pulled the grumpalump.
The lump still grumped.

The bear stared,
the cat sat, the mole
rolled, the dove shoved,
the bull pulled and the yak whacked
the grumpalump.
The lump still grumped.

The bear stared, the cat sat,
the mole rolled, the dove shoved,
the bull pulled, the yak whacked
and the armadillo
used it for a pillow.
But the lump still
grumped.

Then the
gnu blew.

The lump grew plump, and got
humps and bumps, bits and bobs
and interesting knobs,
and wings and things
attached with strings.
And still the
gnu blew.

89

Then, to everyone's surprise,
the grumpalump began to rise.
The gnu drew breath and clambered in.
The grumpalump began to grin.
"I'm off on a trip in my hot airship,"
said the gnu, and flew.
Absolutely true.

And how the bear stared.

Hello, Goodbye

A tree stood quietly
in the sunshine.
A big brown bear
stepped up.

Hello!

"Hello!" he said,
very loudly.

Two bees flew over.
"Hello! Hello!"
they said, very busily.
Along came a big
red bird.
What did the bird say?
"Hello!" – very quickly.
Soon voices all over the
tree were saying, "Hello!"
Little voices on the leaves
said, "Hello!"
Squeaky voices on the
branches said, "Hello!"
Deep-down voices among
the roots said, "Hello!"

hello!

Hello!

by David Lloyd
illustrated by Louise Voce

Goodbye!

Suddenly a drop of rain
fell on the bear's nose.
Splash!
Raindrops fell all
over the bear.
Splash! Splash! Splash!
"Goodbye! Goodbye!"
said the two bees,
very busily.
"Goodbye!" said the big
red bird, very quickly.
What did all the voices
on the tree say?
What did the bear say,
very loudly?
"Goodbye!"
Everyone had gone.
The tree stood
quietly again.
"Hello, rain!" it said,
very, very quietly.

93